MW00887492

MAC'S ADVENTURES
BOOK 1

Mac's Adventures presents a children's book series introducing the funny antics of a Miniature Schnauzer named Mac. The series merges a heartfelt love of dogs, with a child's need for excitement and accomplishment. Through the spirit of a determined little dog, children can discover new ideas about setting goals and never giving up.

MAC'S CURE FOR BOREDOM

Written by Carol McManus   Illustrated by Marc Tobin

"MOM! I'm bored and never have anything to do," whined Mac.
Mom sighed and said, "Mac, you already have a dog door that opens
to the back yard." Mac whimpered, "I know I can always go outside
and chase lots of furry animals, but what I really want to do is have
new adventures like I read about in my library books!"

After digging another big hole in the yard, Dad shouted, "MAC! Put your dog toys in the car!" I panted, "I hope Dad isn't taking me to the Vet!"

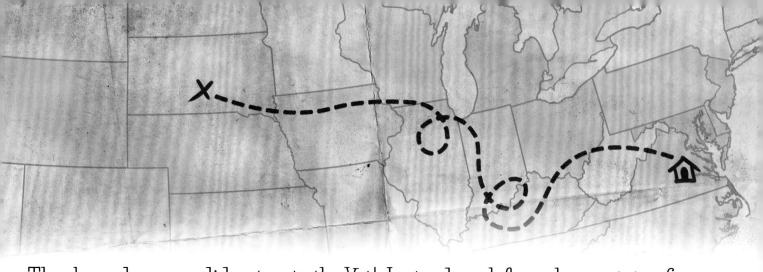

Thank goodness we did not go to the Vet! Instead, we left our home state of Virginia and drove long curvy highways to the state of South Dakota. On day four, I whined to Dad, "I feel car sick, my beard is stuck on my face, and I am very hot!"

Mom gave me "the look" and said, "MAC! Move your paw off that window button and get your head back inside this car!"

We finally arrived in South Dakota and stopped at a rest area for another walk. I looked around and woofed, "Wow! Look at that statue! Her name tag says she is Dignity of Earth and Sky." Just then, Dad whistled for me to get back into the car. I said, "Don't worry, Dignity, I'm staying right here until you talk to me."

After Dad assisted me back into the car, we drove along until I saw four gigantic heads on top of a mountain. Dad explained, "That carving is part of the Mount Rushmore National Memorial, and the heads represent 4 past American Presidents." I replied, "Do all Presidents have big heads?"

"Hey parents! You forgot to wake me up from my nap and it turned into night," I cried. Mom ignored my whining and said, "Look at the carving, Mac. That is the Native American leader, named Crazy Horse, who is watching over the burial ground of his ancestors." I yelped, "Wow! His face is glowing from the light of the full Moon! I Love That Moon!"

Mom and Dad said I whined too much in the car, so we headed
back to Virginia to pick up our little airplane so we could travel
faster. As we drove through the state of Indiana, I looked up and
shouted, "Mom! Dad! Check out the beautiful balloons in the sky!
I wonder if they have room for dogs in those baskets?"

Oh no! I decided to sneak a ride in one of the balloons and it floated really fast in the direction of Virginia! I shouted down to Mom and Dad chasing me in the car, "HELP!! If I make it to our little airport, I promise to be a good boy and wait for you beside our airplane!"

After a hard landing of my hot air balloon near our airplane hangar, I met my parents beside the plane. Mom and Dad both agreed our first flight should be to the state of Florida to see a rocket launch at Cape Canaveral. I woofed, "Yay! WAIT! What does rocket mean?" Dad shouted, "Look straight ahead, Mac!"

Rocket Launch

NASA Assembly Building

Then Mom said, "Look at the Kennedy Space Center! It has
exhibits you can touch, and astronaut training classes. We will
visit there soon, but first, let's go meet your first cat and guinea
pig." I barked, "Yay! WAIT! What does cat and guinea pig mean?"

Well, I found out the Cat was HUGE, had glowing green eyes, and orange fur.

Come here little doggie so we can play swat!

I surrender, Cat!!

Hey! I'm just the little guinea pig minding my own business.

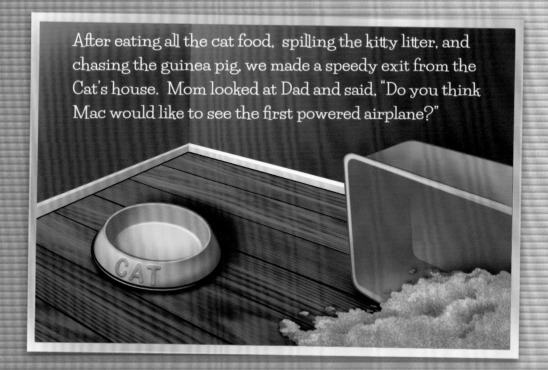

After eating all the cat food, spilling the kitty litter, and chasing the guinea pig, we made a speedy exit from the Cat's house. Mom looked at Dad and said, "Do you think Mac would like to see the first powered airplane?"

IMAGINE

WILBUR
WRIGHT
ORVILLE
WRIGHT

IN COMMEMORATION OF THE CONQUEST OF THE AIR BY

ORVILLE

WILBUR

I asked Mom, "Who are Wilbur and Orville Wright?"
Mom explained, "They are the two brothers who invented and flew
the world's first powered airplane on December 17, 1903. The winds
were very cold that day and the longest flight lasted 12 seconds.

Whoops, I whimpered, "I'm really sorry that I forgot to read the sign about no digging in the National Park. The dirt in front of the Wright Brothers' Flyer looked so nice and soft!"

Please Use Sidewalks

🚲 Bicycles

🛹 Skateboards

🛼 Rollerblades

🪏 Digging

This Means You Mac!

The parents shouted together, "MAC!!"
Then Dad said, "We are flying back to Virginia before you get into more trouble!" I woofed with glee, "YES! I'm finally going back home!"

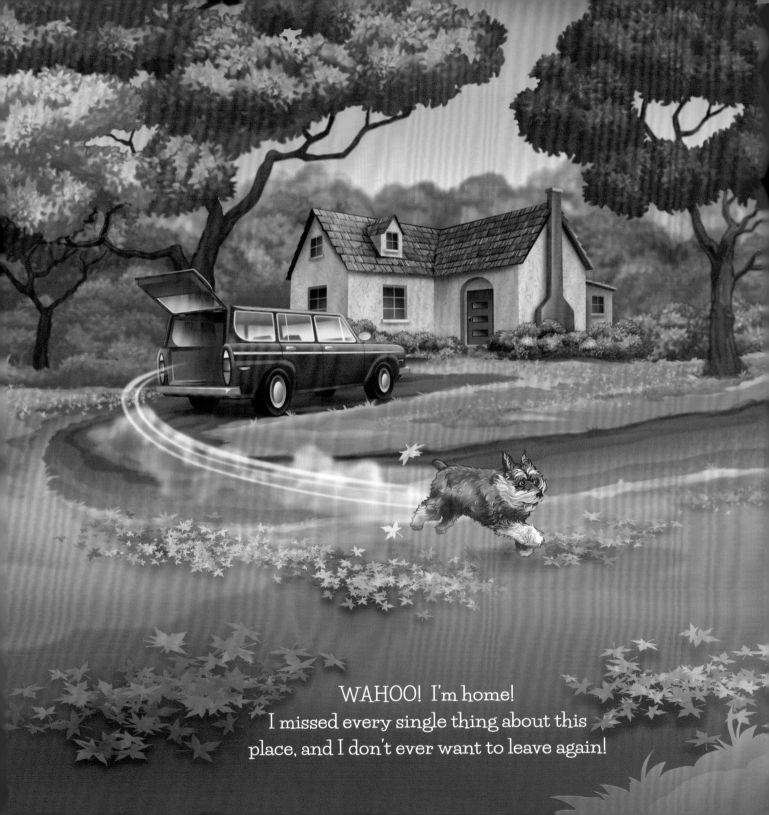

WAHOO! I'm home!
I missed every single thing about this
place, and I don't ever want to leave again!

WAIT! I just had a brilliant idea!
I know how to keep myself busy, stay out
of trouble, and never be bored again!

"Mom! Dad! I need one of you to take me to the library right away, I panted! My next big adventure is inside one of their books!"

WOW! A Book About The Moon. I really LOVE the Moon!

BOOK ABOUT THE MOON

HUH! I could really be the first dog on the MOON!
Astronaut training here I come!

Acknowledgements

Carol A. McManus

Carol is the author of the new children's book titled, Mac's Cure For Boredom. This book is the first of a series starring Mac, the Miniature Schnauzer. Carol is retired from Civil Service and lives with her husband and dog in Yorktown, Virginia. She loves traveling, taking digital photos, and playing games with her grandchildren.

Brookhaven's California Cracker. Mac

Mac is a registered Miniature Schnauzer born in California to champion show dogs. Mom flew with Mac on a plane to his new home in Virginia when he was 4 months old. He loves playing with humans of all sizes, taking long walks, and chasing squirrels and rabbits that he never catches. He also loves posing for the camera at every opportunity.

Additional Facts About My New Discoveries

Dignity of Earth & Sky is a 50 ft. high stainless-steel statue given as a gift from Norm and Eunabel McKie of Rapid City, South Dakota, in 2014. The statue honors the 125th anniversary of South Dakota statehood, and stands near Chamberlain, South Dakota, at the Welcome Center located near Interstate 90, mile post 264.

Hot air balloons float by increasing the air temperature inside the nylon envelope making it less dense than the surrounding (ambient) air. Hot air is pumped into the balloon envelope by using a burner unit that gasifies liquid propane, mixes it with air, ignites the mixture, and directs the flame and exhaust into the mouth of the envelope causing the balloon to rise.

Cape Canaveral is a point of land located in Brevard County, Florida, near the center of the state's Atlantic coast. It was known as Cape Kennedy from 1963 to 1973 and the area is part of a region now known as the Space Coast and home of the Cape Canaveral Air Force Station. Several rocket launch pads are located there, including those operated by NASA and SpaceX.

Websites Referenced

DIGNITY STATUE - Wikipedia
https://en.wikipedia.org/wiki/dignity (statue)
https://www.creativecommons.org
Creative Commons Attribution Share-Alike License (CC-BY-SA-4.0)

HOT AIR BALLOONS - Explain That Stuff
https://www.explainthatstuff.com ›how-hot-air-balloons-work
Woodford, Chris (2011/2019) Hot Air Balloons, Retrieved

CAPE CANAVERAL - Wikipedia
https://en.wikipedia.org/Cape_Canaveral
https:creativecommons.org
Creative Commons Attribution Share-Alike License (CC-BY-SA-4.0)
ASTRONAUT TRAINING EXPERIENCE (ATX)
https://www.kennedyspacecenter.com/explore-attractions/all-attractions/mars-base-1

Mac's Adventures Series

Mac's Moon Dream Comes True

Book 2
Mac's Moon Dream Comes True is the humorous story
of a Miniature Schnauzer with a dream of becoming
the first dog on the Moon. Mac's Mom tries to tell him
only human astronauts get to travel in spaceships
to the Moon, but he mails his application to NASA
anyway. When NASA accepts him for training, his best
adventure unfolds as he becomes an astronaut and goes
to the Moon!

ISBNs:
Hardback: 979-8-9852352-2-7
Paperback: 979-8-9852352-3-4

Mac's Adventures Series

Mac Forgot to Follow Directions
(And Ended Up On Mars)

Book 3

Mac's hilarious adventures continue as this funny little dog forgets to follow directions while living with the First Woman on the Moon for 2 years. When it is time for him to return to Earth, his love of baseball distracts him, he takes a wrong turn at the "Y" in a road, and ends up on a starship to Mars. Humorous situations are non-stop on the starship as he is trapped for 7 months on this eventful trip.

ISBNs:
Hardback: 979-8-9852352-4-1
Paperback: 979-8-9852352-5-8

Mac's Adventures Series books are available in Hardback, Paperback, and eBooks through your favorite bookseller.

DEDICATION
Thank you to our pets who give us unconditional love throughout their years.
A special thank you to Mac, for his endless energy and constant antics.
And to Mr. Bear, his cat friend, who left us too soon.

©Copyright 2022 by Carol McManus
Text Copyright 2022 by Carol McManus
Illustration Copyright 2022 by Carol McManus

All rights reserved. No part of this publication may be reproduced or
transmitted in any form or by any means, without permission in writing
from the author.

Printed in China, First Edition, 2022

ISBN: 979-8-9852352-1-0
Library of Congress Control Number: 2021922924